O Lord my God, I will give you thanks forever.

Psalm 30:12

Thankful Together

To Mom and Dad, for whom I'm thankful.
—H.D.

In memory of my grandmother Eugenia Sokolova-Tverjanovich.
—V.S.

Text © 2003 Holly C. Davis. Illustrations © 2003 Valerie Sokolova.

© 2003 Standard Publishing, Cincinnati, Ohio. A division of Standex International Corporation. All rights reserved.

Sprout logo is a trademark of Standard Publishing. Printed in Italy.

Project editor: Jennifer Holder. Cover and interior design: Robert Glover.

Scripture taken from the HOLY BIBLE, NEW INTERNATIONAL VERSION®. NIV®.

Copyright © 1973, 1978, 1984 by International Bible Society.

Used by permission of Zondervan. All rights reserved.

ISBN 0-7847-1436-3

10 09 08 07 06 05 04   9 8 7 6 5 4 3 2

Thankful Together

written by *Holly Davis*

illustrated by *Valerie Sokolova*

STANDARD PUBLISHING
CINCINNATI, OHIO

When you wake in the morning,
I'll come to your side,
Peek under the sheet
Where small sleepyheads hide.

We'll pull up the blind
From your window to see
The sky, swept of night,
And the sun through the tree.

Thank you, God,
For the wonderful morning.

When we put on your shirt,
You'll poke your head through,
I'll give you a wink
And say, "Peek-a-boo!"

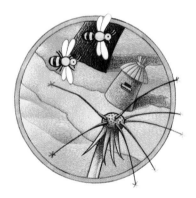

"Would there be a bosky dell hereabouts?"

"This O.K. with knackwurst?"

"But the Taj Mahal was ticky-tacky, I thought."

"I didn't say God is dead. I simply said that my hubcaps were lifted while I attended church."

"Hold it! Hold it! I'm a responsible representative, and this is a divergent view."

"Would you go ahead of me? I can't seem to get my dander up."

"I wouldn't call two Gesundheit's in seven years a sincere effort to communicate."

"*Hey, Martha! Guess what!*"

"*I haven't the heart to tell them it has stopped transmitting.*"

"I'd like to point out that there are people trying to listen
to a message of importance in here."

"Watch who you're calling irrelevant!"

"Welcome to Expo 07."

"Harlan, some booze for Dr. Bassett."

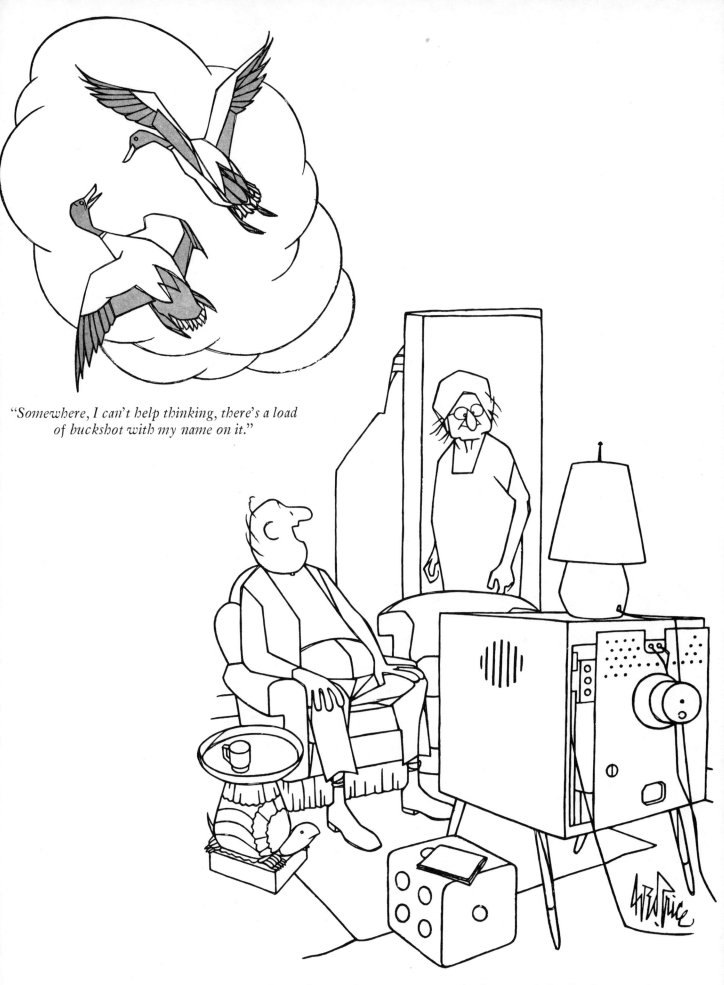

"*Somewhere, I can't help thinking, there's a load of buckshot with my name on it.*"

"*Just when you're once again beginning to feel that life has passed you by, here comes another television first.*"

"*She gave me a come-hither look, I went thither, and the rest is history.*"

"*When hootenanny beckons us, we're ready.*"

"Come, come, now! Prime time, everybody!"

"And now, from the distaff side, an editorial
opinion on the same subject."

"Erskine, you know that different drummer
you're always marching to?"

"How do you spell 'preamble'?"

"Let me put it this way. Exhibited behind bullet-proof glass it'll never be."

"I believe I'll take the baked-meatloaf trip."

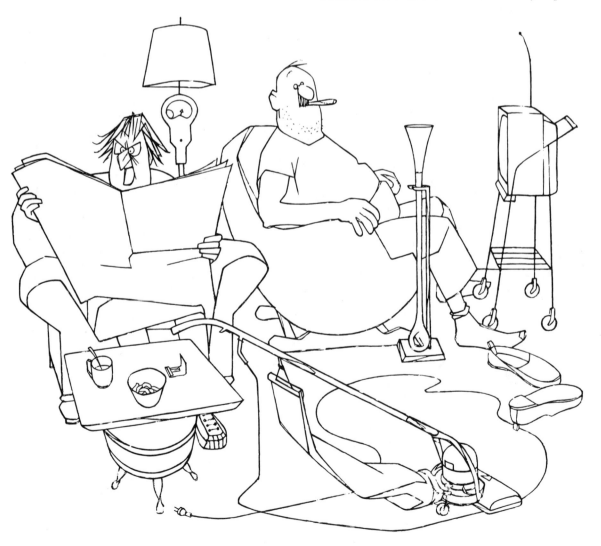

"Damn! Last week was Take Your Wife Out to Dinner Week!"

"*I never promised you a rose garden.*"

"*Well, so far his behavior has been exemplary.*"

*"About four months ago, he had a room added to the house,
and I haven't laid eyes on him since."*

"Sorry, folks.
The chef just threw in the towel on the boiled tripe à la Grecque."

"That eleven-o'clock crowd never fails to ring my chimes."

"To be repaid in full in twelve months.
We're not interested in lifelong friendships."

"Have you got a minute to help me compose a crank letter?"

"We'll call you back after nine. We're in the middle of the Family Hour."

"*Grab a beaker, Heubner! This breakthrough is big enough for both of us!*"

"These days, everybody is looking for answers."

*"Just when you think he's completely cockeyed,
he comes up with another one of those damn aphorisms."*

"Just rooms? No efficiencies?"

"Belly up, Bradburn. I want you to hear me, and hear me good!"

"She's been a lot easier to live with since the bottom dropped out of her ESP."

"He didn't really die of anything. He was a hypochondriac."

"My mother doesn't even bother to come to the games."

"*It's some odd-ball salesman.*"

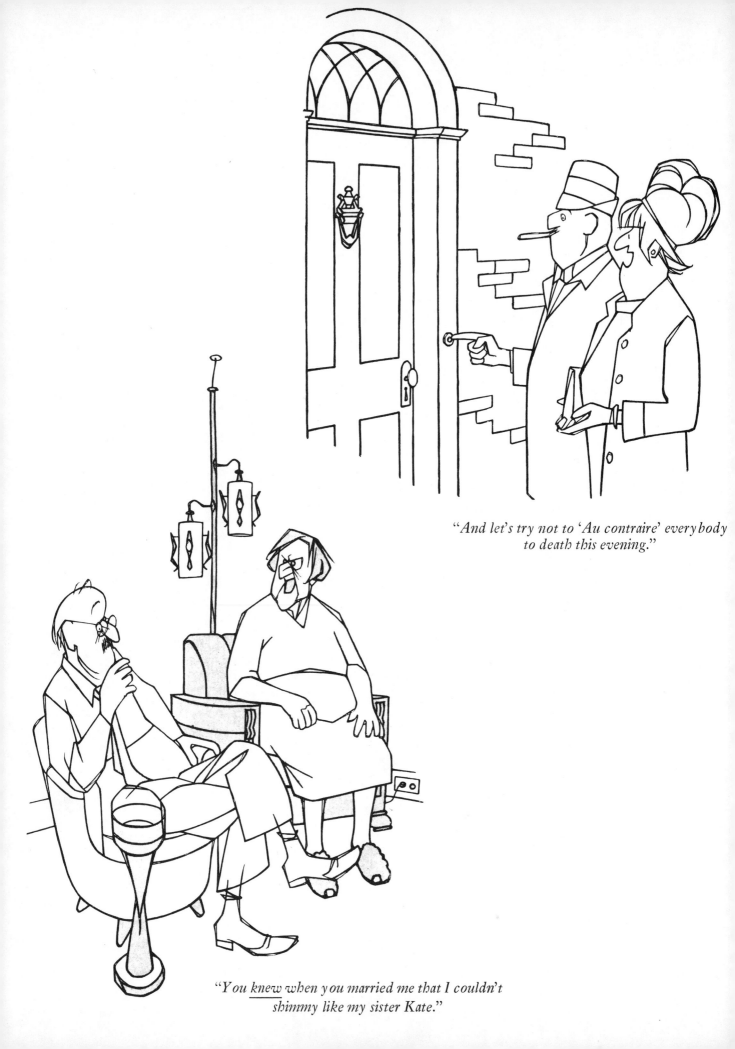

"And let's try not to 'Au contraire' everybody to death this evening."

"You <u>knew</u> when you married me that I couldn't shimmy like my sister Kate."

"*This year we're not missing the fun of indoor gardening.*"

"Ralph! Do we need money?"

"*Well! This looks like an idea whose time has come!*"

"*Anything yet from your ESP on the whereabouts of the bay leaves?*"

"This must be the last family bar in the Bronx."

*"Having the whitest wash on the block, week after week—surely
there must be more to life than that."*

*"And that's the last time I get conned into saying grace
over a Tomato Surprise."*

*"Friends, we have temporarily lost the video portion of our talk show but
will continue to bring you the inane flummery of our panelists."*

" 'Body all achin' an' racked wid pain . . .' "

"No, no! The day the earth stood still was in May. We weren't married till June."

"*For goodness' sake, can't I raise the teeniest objection to our foreign policy without you waving that flag in my face?*"

"*Well, you certainly look relaxed. What the hell is that all about?*"

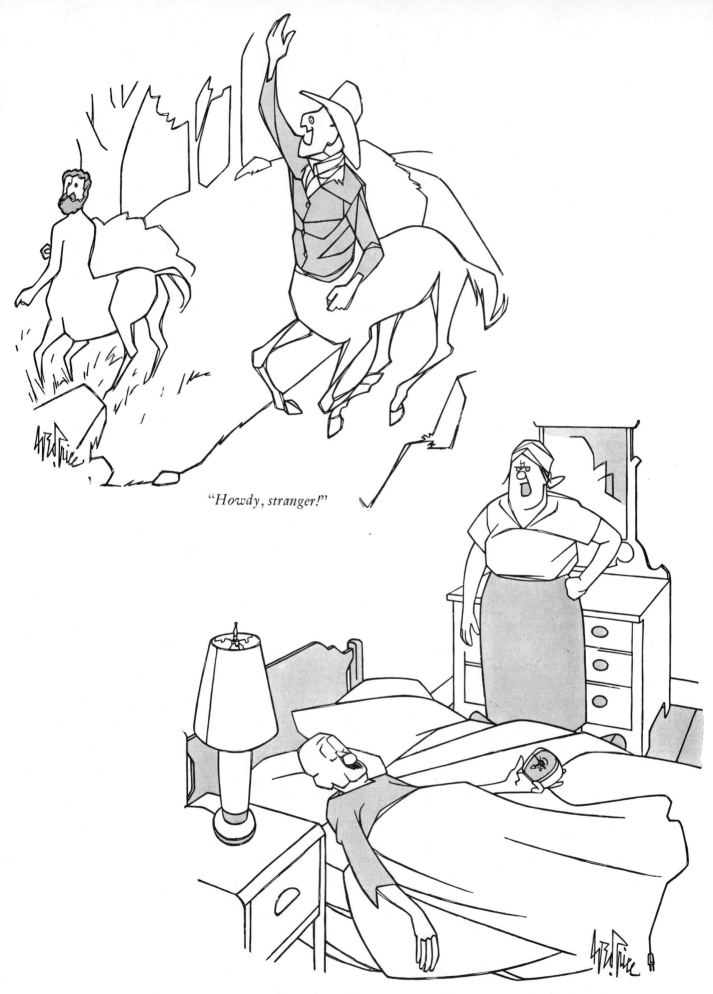

"Howdy, stranger!"

"Would it help if I belted out a chorus of 'You Are My Sunshine'?"

"*Easter was last week.*"

"*And about those damn alligators you keep in the basement,
let me quote from an Ann Landers column of Tuesday last.*"

"*Lord, how you must have suffered!*"

"Al Disbrow? I believe he went into the V.I.P. Lounge."

*"As far as the management of this store is concerned,
Madam, yours is a voice crying in the wilderness."*

*"Those people who said our marriage would never last should
know we've gone through three picture tubes already."*

"We'll have been married forty-one years come Tuesday. Don't you think it's high time you showed your true colors?"

"Will you lay on the Boilermakers or shall I?"

"Is this cabin pressurized properly? My baked apple just blew up."

"I *said*, you're standing on my metatarsals."

"You damn well did not mention
that they had a gifted child!"

"Indoor-outdoor carpeting?"

"We merged to save through volume buying."

"This has always been a popular spot with the sports crowd."

"O.K., gang. Let's hear it for Mr. Kirby."

"It is an old ticker,
isn't it?"

"You're going to quote me out of context
just once too often."

"*Well, how is this too, too solid flesh this morning?*"

"Which way to the House of Good Taste, Mac?"

"*Hi, Midge! My encounter group decided to come along for dinner.*"

"... and if nominated I will not run, and if elected I will not serve."

"And you say black is the color of your true love's hair?"

"You needn't go to all this trouble to put the magic back
into our marriage on _my_ account."

"We were stompin' at the Savoy, our eyes met across the room, and that was it."

"And as a consequence the silver-bell tinkle has gone out of my laughter."

"You remembered the day!"

"Good morning. Over and out."

"*What are we watching? We're watching 'Lancer,' Jerry Lewis, and 'Mod Squad.'*"

"Hey, pal! Care to hire an entourage?"

*"The sneer is gone from Casey's lips,
his teeth are clenched in hate."*

"Let's go, Mets!"

"Look, do you want to hear this
cock-and-bull story or don't you?"

"You'll have to speak up. Your estimate blew my hearing aid."

"That's my Horace in 1957, just before he lost his train of thought."

"At what hour tomorrow do you wish to resume your humdrum existence?"

"How dare you crank me up for stewed apricots!"

"Between the 'Ho, ho, ho's' and the 'Bah, humbug's' I've about had it."

"*The last time I saw him, he was heading across the lawn on his seven-horsepower, thirty-two-inch, heavy-duty Craftsman rotary mower.*"

"*Was it something I averred?*"

"Did you see a walking sprinkler go by here?"

"Were there any important messages for the men in the audience while I was out?"

"*An eighty-seven! You must have
worn your Arnold Palmer all-weather sports jacket!*"

"*Also, we come to socialize—not to tie one on.*"

"*On the afternoon of September fourth, nineteen sixty-nine, he had one for the road, and that was the last I ever saw of him.*"

"As long as you're Grant, get me a 7-Up."

"Are they biting at Sparrow Lake?"

"Set seven places for dinner, Sweetie. I brought home some friends."

"O.K., so happy anniversary—over and out."

"Hon, would you stand up a minute? I want Mr. Ellengast to see your regal bearing."

"Wilbur, please come home! The children ask for you."

"I understand they're a ménage à trois."

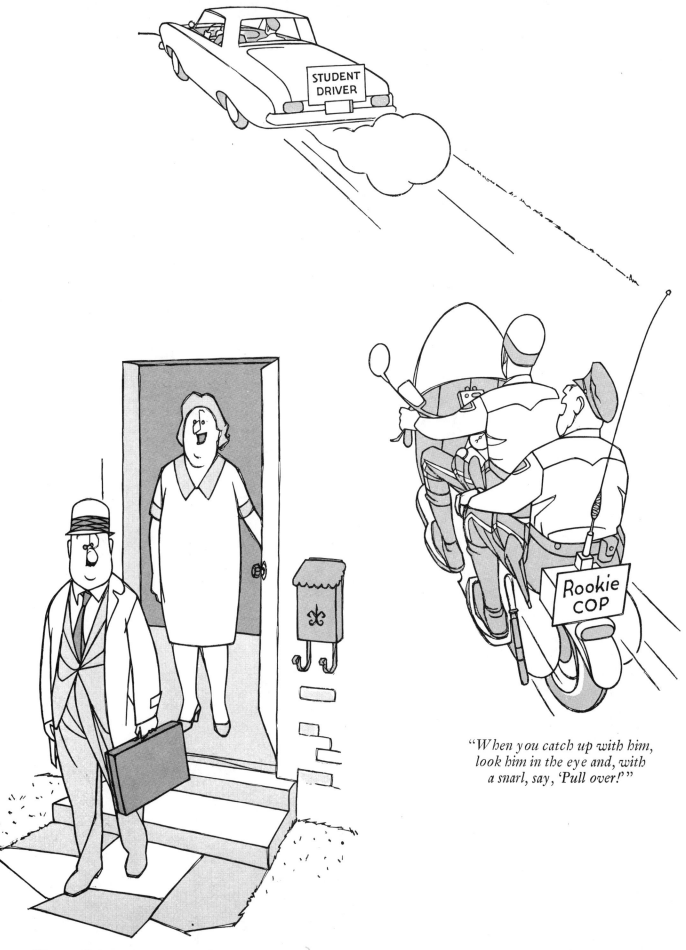

"When you catch up with him, look him in the eye and, with a snarl, say, 'Pull over!'"

"Farewell, brave lover! Come back either with your shield or upon it."

"If you believe in Euell Gibbons,
clap your hands."

"No breakfast this morning, a lousy cup of bouillon for lunch,
and now you tell me I've been voted out of the family plot!"

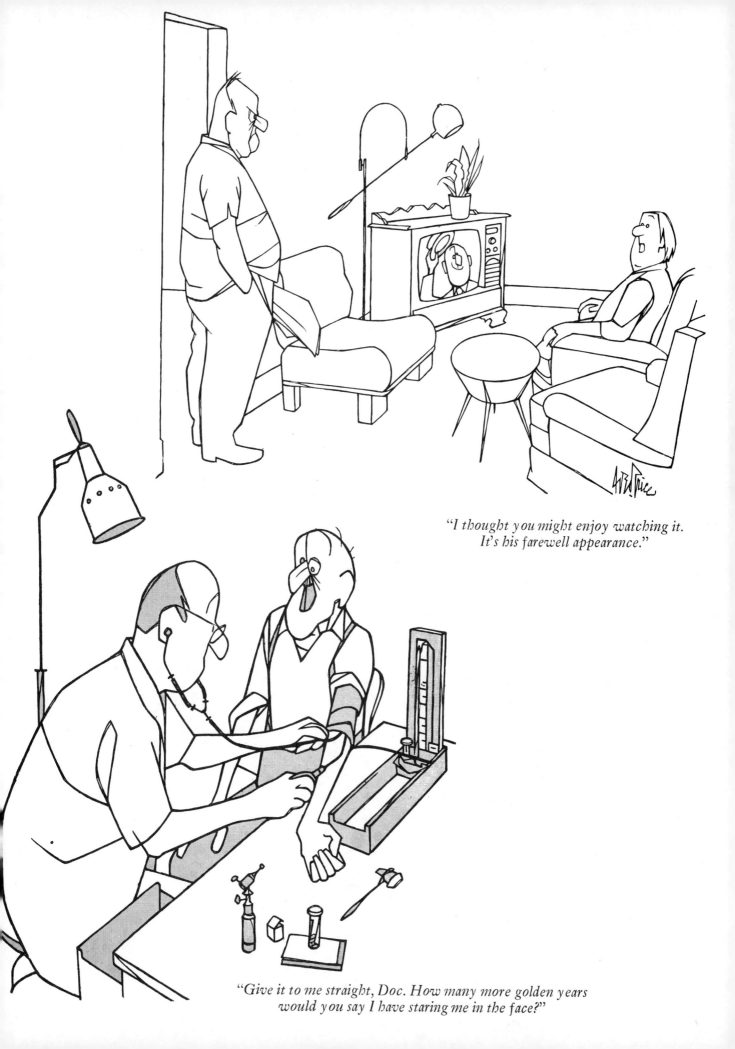

"I thought you might enjoy watching it.
It's his farewell appearance."

"Give it to me straight, Doc. How many more golden years
would you say I have staring me in the face?"

"I thought you might enjoy it.
It's that old Bette Davis flick
where she gets one right across the chops."

"I did not say it wasn't a super-shot. I merely said that I, personally, was not electrified."

"I have this recurring dream about reclining
on a bed of wild rice."

"It's Julia Child's cutlets with Galloping Gourmet sauce."

"*Don't ask me which fork. You bought the sweepstakes ticket.*"

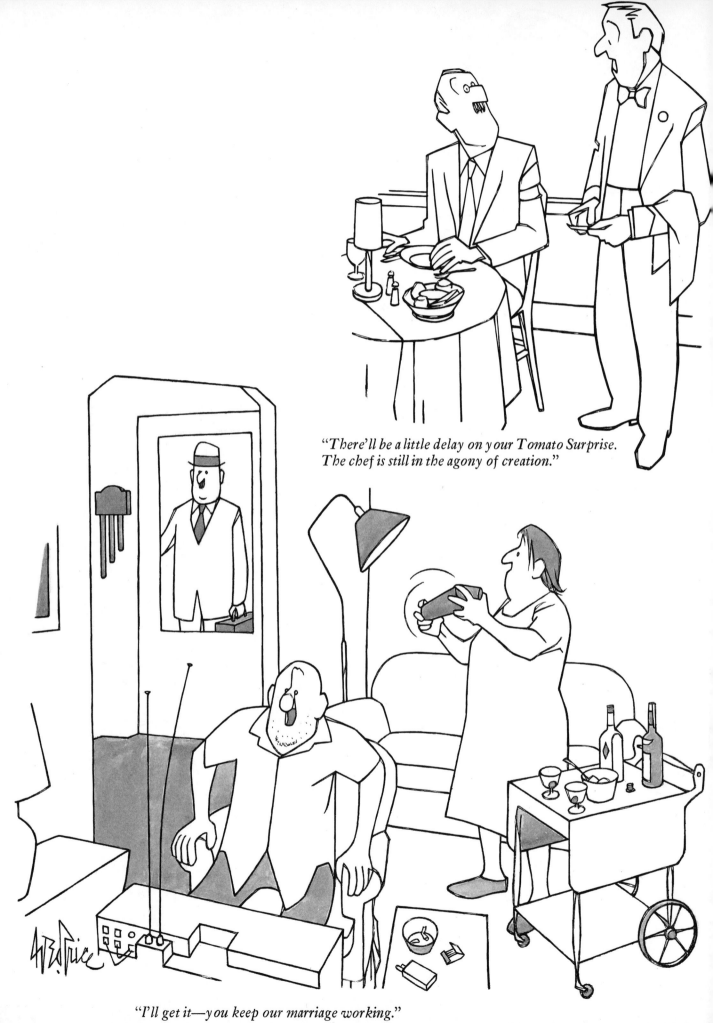

"There'll be a little delay on your Tomato Surprise. The chef is still in the agony of creation."

"I'll get it—you keep our marriage working."

"I said, 'Dinner's ready.'"

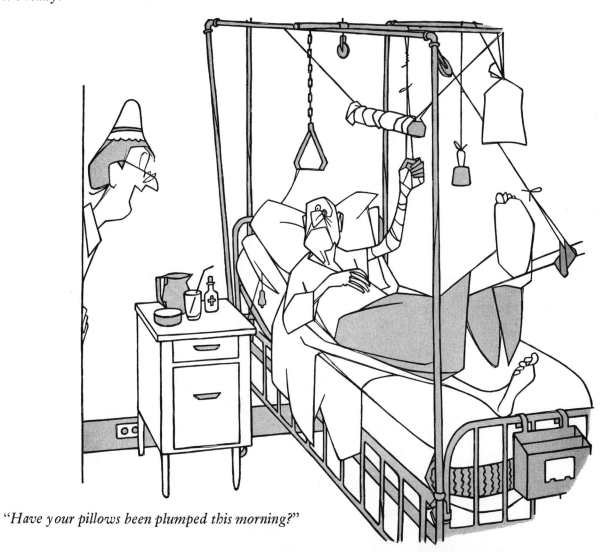

"Have your pillows been plumped this morning?"

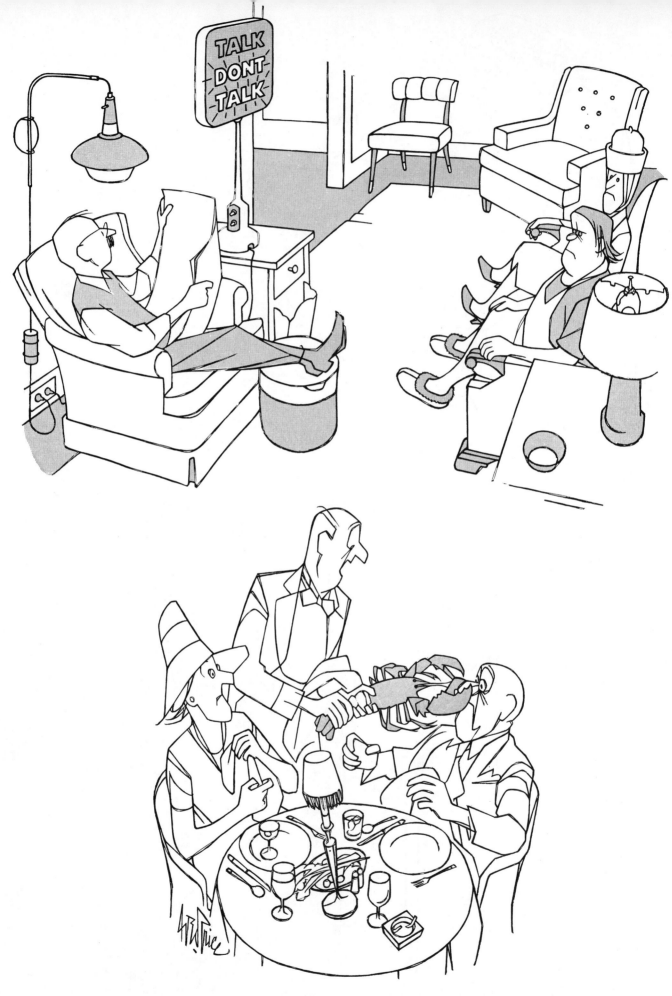

"Oh, I'm sorry. It's just another instance of senseless violence."

"Aloha!"

"*Twenty-seven birds to choose from and we come up with a raconteur!*"

"What's your bag?
Novocain or Sodium Pentothal?"

"I like the way Harper slugs it out with them on their own level."

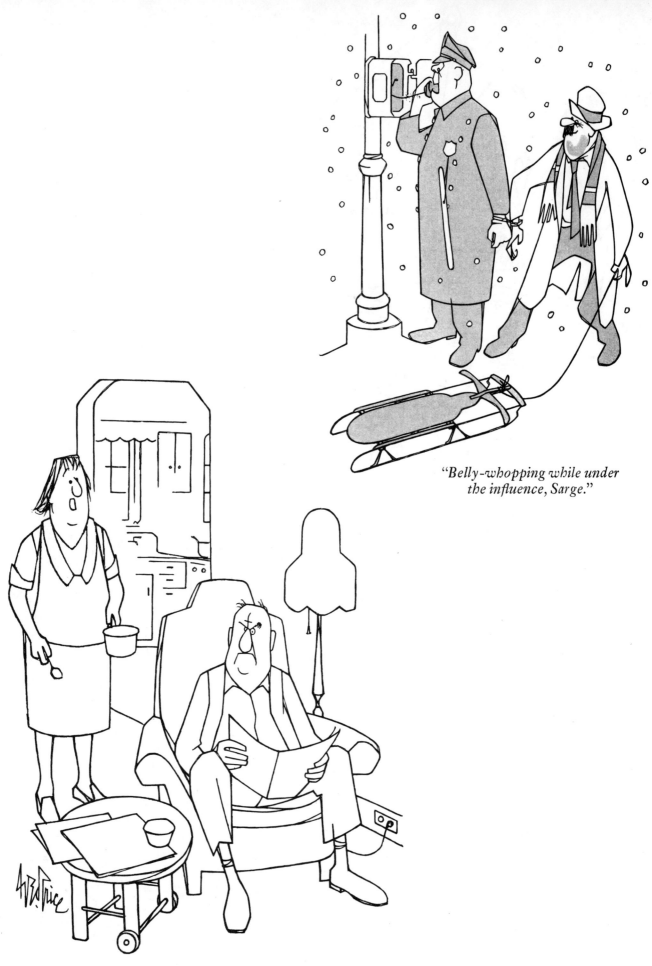

"Belly-whopping while under
the influence, Sarge."

"Refresh my memory. Is it creamed spinach that billows your sails,
and creamed asparagus that leaves you dead in the water? Or vice versa?"

"Tell me this, Mrs. Osterman. After knocking you down, does he proceed to a neutral corner?"

"And one other thing. I'd stay out of that old conversation pit for a while."

"*Do you stock Melhauser's 'Book of Genteel Profanities'?*"

"You'll like Charlie's.
The bouncer has a glass jaw."

"The tumult and the shouting dies;
The captains and the kings depart."

"Lost in the magic of your kiss, I forgot about the potato salad. Bring home a quart."

"'Us'"

"It's good to hear you laugh again."

"For dessert, we have Twinkies, Hostess cupcakes, or Devil Dogs."

"I can't get a peep out of him.
You sure he went down the tube?"

"Ding! Dong! Your toast is done, through the courtesy of the Citizens'
National Bank, which pays six per cent on Investor's Passbook accounts."

"Anything you want from the cellar before I settle down?"

"Will you be right home after the peccadillo?"

"Damn him!
Those were to be _my_ last words!"

"Do you mind terribly if we end another evening on a sour note?"

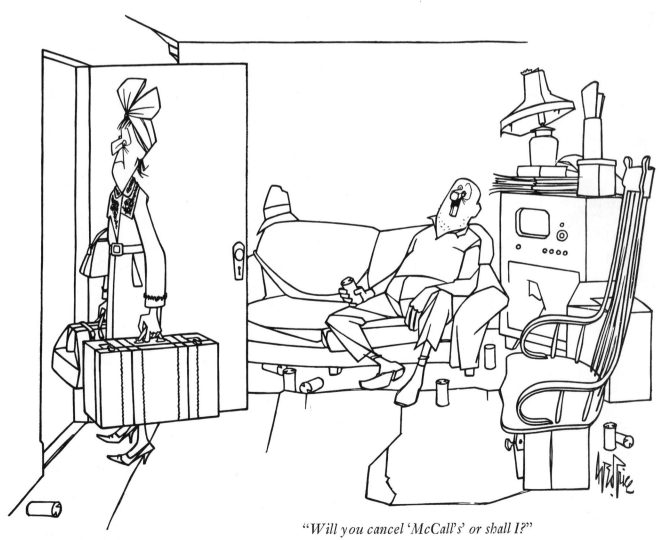

"Will you cancel 'McCall's' or shall I?"

"If it says 'Clearing by midmorning,' stand back!"

"I'm sorry, sir. To take advantage of our student rates one must be between twelve and twenty-nine."

"The saints preserve us."

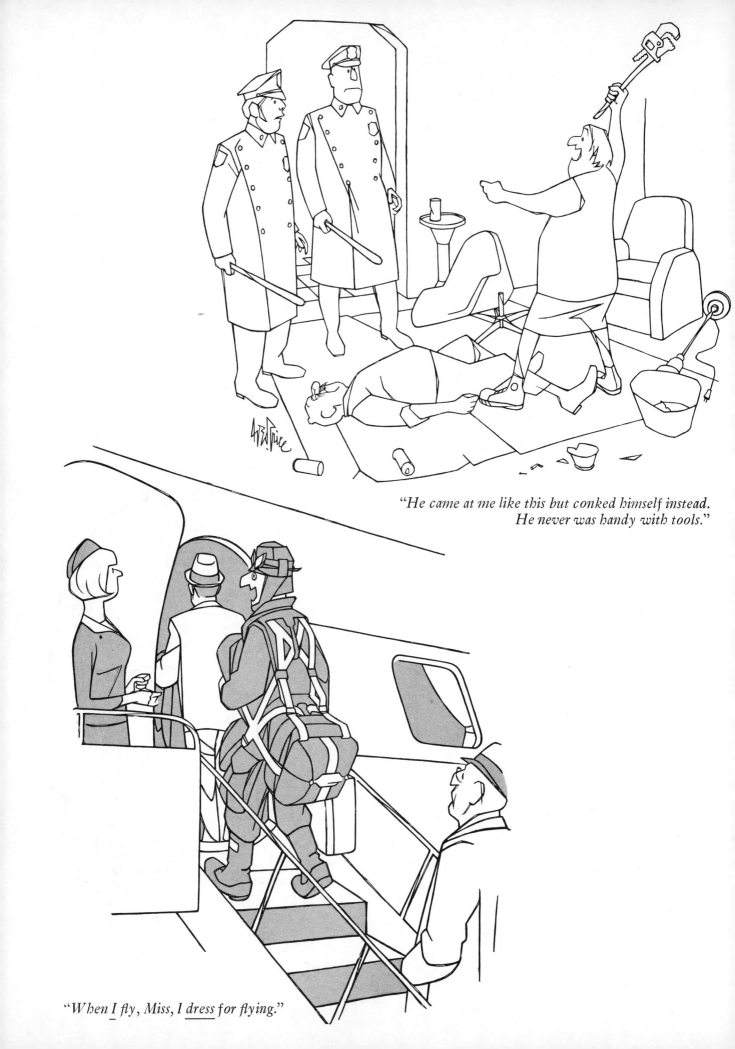

"He came at me like this but conked himself instead.
He never was handy with tools."

"When _I_ fly, Miss, I _dress_ for flying."

"May I join you?"

" 'Wild Kingdom'—pretty tame. 'Revenge of the Mole People'—small bore. 'World of Disney'—Mickey Mouse. 'Mystery Theatre'—the butler did it. 'Lawrence Welk'—flat. 'Court Music of the Fourteenth Century'—next case. 'Estrellas de Buenos Aires'—South America, take it away."

"He's one of those people who need people."

"Any word as to the nature of the soupe du jour?"

"*Could we come back tomorrow? We're still two for,
two against, and one undecided.*"

"*The missus will be down shortly. She's getting her act together.*"

"*Visiting hours are over, Mrs. Glenhorn.*"

"Thank you. You're aging gracefully yourself."

"It's amazing. After ninety-three years of carrying on, his chickens
still haven't come home to roost."

"You are silent. Am I to assume
that you do not have a child who can do every bit as well?"

"It won't be long now, sir. The kitchen is a beehive of activity."